visit us at www.abdopublishing.com

Reinforced library bound edition published in 2014 by Spotlight, a division of the ABDO Group, PO Box 398166, Minneapolis, MN 55439. Spotlight produces high-quality reinforced library bound editions for schools and libraries. Published by agreement with Grosset & Dunlap, a division of Penguin Young Readers Group.

Printed in the United States of America, North Mankato, Minnesota.
102013
012014

 This book contains at least 10% recycled materials.

Library of Congress Cataloging-in-Publication Data
This title was previously cataloged with the following information:

Krulik, Nancy E.
Three burps and you're out! / by Nancy Krulik ; illustrated by Aaron Blecha.
  p. cm. -- (George Brown, Class Clown)
  Summary: George is the catcher for the school baseball team, but when they play their archrivals in the championship game, will a magical super burp lead the Sugarman Sea Monkeys to victory or defeat?
  [1. Behavior--Fiction. 2. Belching--Fiction. 3. Baseball--Fiction. 4. Schools--Fiction. 5. Magic--Fiction.] I. Title. II Series.
  PZ7.K9416 Thn 2013
  [Fic]--dc23   2012034688

ISBN 978-1-61479-220-8 (Reinforced Library Bound Edition)

All Spotlight books are reinforced library binding
and manufactured in the United States of America.

For Ian, my homerun kid!–NK

For Ed and Al - Grandpas that are missed–AB

George Brown, CLASS CLOWN

Three Burps and You're Out!

by Nancy Krulik

illustrated by Aaron Blecha

Grosset & Dunlap
An Imprint of Penguin Group (USA) Inc.

Chapter 1

"Swing and a miss! Strike one!" Coach Trainer called out.

George Brown frowned as the baseball soared over the plate and right past his bat. **How'd he miss that one?** He'd kept his eyes on the ball and swung level—everything Coach Trainer had told him to do.

"Ha-ha!" Louie Farley laughed from the bench. "The only way you're gonna hit that ball is with your big head!"

"Cut it out, Louie," George's friend Julianna said. "It's only batting practice. We're all on the same team. Remember?"

Louie rolled his eyes. "I've been

trying to forget that all afternoon."

"Good joke, Louie," his friend Mike told him.

"You're the **king of comedy**!" Louie's other friend, Max, added.

George shook his head. Max and Mike were so wrong. That hadn't been a good joke. It hadn't even *been* a joke.

Coach Trainer picked up another ball and got ready to pitch it to George. "Let's try this again," he said.

"Okay," George replied. "I'm ready."

The coach let the baseball fly from the pitcher's mound. George kept his eyes focused on the little white ball as it came closer. He got ready to swing. And then . . .

CRACK!

George hit the ball and sent it flying over Coach Trainer's head.

"Yes!" George exclaimed.

"Awesome, dude!" George's best friend, Alex, cheered.

"Good job," Coach Trainer told him. "Hitting like that'll bring the Edith B. Sugarman Elementary Sea Monkeys **the championship trophy**."

George grinned. There was nothing his school team wanted more than to win the championship game against their archrivals, the Klockermeister Elementary Kangaroos. The Sea Monkeys had only lost one game all season. That gave them a record of 9–1. Which would have been great— if their only loss hadn't been to the Klockermeister Kangaroos.

This time, though, George's team was determined to beat those Kangaroos and win the championship. That was why they were practicing so hard on a Friday afternoon. The game was just **one week away**.

Coach Trainer walked to the dugout where the team was sitting during batting practice. "But before we can win anything, we have to work on some fielding skills," he told them. "So everyone, take your spots. I'll hit to you."

The kids jumped off the bench and started running to their positions. Alex ran to right field. George's other pal, Chris, headed over to the left. Julianna got on the pitcher's mound. Mike went to first base, and Max headed to shortstop.

Louie started to put on his catcher's equipment. George was on his way to third base when suddenly **Louie's mom raced onto the field**.

"Wait a minute!" Mrs. Farley shouted.

Everyone stopped moving. George hadn't even noticed that Mrs. Farley had been there watching. Parents weren't supposed to come to practices. That was the rule. But Louie's mom didn't think

rules applied to the Farley family.

"I thought I told you Louie wasn't going to be the catcher anymore," Mrs. Farley said to Coach Trainer.

Coach Trainer shook his head. "You suggested that, but I thought . . ."

"I don't like the way the mask covers my Loo Loo Poo's face," Mrs. Farley continued.

George cracked up. *Loo Loo Poo*. Man, that was **classic**.

"I think Louie would do better at third base," Mrs. Farley told the coach. "That was one of the positions his brother, Sam, played two years ago. Which, I'll point out, was the last time the Sugarman Sea Monkeys won a championship."

Coach Trainer sighed.

George could tell he was getting tired of fighting Louie's mom. Not that George blamed him. Mrs. Farley always got what she wanted. So what was the point in fighting her?

"Okay. I'll try Louie at third," Coach Trainer told Mrs. Farley. He looked out in the field and waved to George. **"Take over as catcher, George."**

"Yes, that will work fine," Mrs. Farley said. She turned and walked back toward the bleachers.

Louie smiled smugly as he handed George the catcher's mask and chest protector. "Coach Trainer is doing the right thing," he said. "I'm a better player than you. And third base is a really important position."

"They're *all* important positions," George said.

"But third base is the MOST

important," Louie told him. "I'm the last stop before home plate."

"I'm going to be the one *at* home plate," George reminded him. "And I have to be ready to catch every ball Julianna pitches. That means I'm going to be part of *every play*. You're going to have to wait until a ball gets hit or is thrown to you."

Louie stopped smiling. He obviously hadn't thought of that.

"Okay, let's get going," Coach Trainer said. "George, are you ready?"

"Oh yeah!" George said as he crouched down behind the plate. Coach Trainer took a bat and stepped up to the plate.

"Okay, Julianna! Pitch me a good one."

Julianna eyed the batter's

box. George pointed four fingers at the ground. That was the signal for a **curveball**. Julianna nodded and let the ball fly.

Crack! Coach Trainer hit the ball solidly. It flew to the left.

"I got it! I got it!" Louie shouted. He reached his glove in the air. "I got it."

Plop. Louie *didn't* have it. In fact, it flew right over his head and **landed in the dirt**.

"That's okay, Louie," Coach Trainer said. "Pick it up, and throw it home."

Louie nodded. He grabbed the ball and threw it with all his might—right at George.

Bam! The ball smacked George right in the chest.

George gasped. It was a good thing he was wearing the thick chest protector. A throw like that could knock the burp right out of a guy. And that would have been awful. Because George knew better than anyone the kind of trouble a burp could cause—especially if it was **a magical super burp**!

It had all started on George's first day at Edith B. Sugarman Elementary School. George's family had moved—again. That meant George was the new kid—again. George's dad was in the army, so his family moved around a lot. It seemed like George was *always* the new kid.

This time, though, George had promised himself that things were going to be different. He was turning over a new leaf. No more pranks. No more class clown. He wasn't going to get into any trouble anymore, like he had at all his old schools.

At first, it really worked. George

didn't make jokes or funny faces in the middle of class. He raised his hand before answering questions. And he didn't laugh behind his teacher's back. That last part was really hard when you had a teacher like Mrs. Kelly, who did stuff like hula dance in the middle of the classroom.

But new George was also boring George. At the end of that first day, the other kids didn't even seem to know he existed. It was as though he was *invisible* George.

That night, George's parents took him out for dessert to cheer him up. While they were sitting outside at the ice cream parlor and George was finishing his root beer float, **a shooting star** flashed across the sky. George made a wish.

I want to make kids laugh—but not get into trouble.

Unfortunately, the star was gone

before George could finish the wish. So only part of it came true—the first part.

A minute later, George had **a funny feeling in his belly**. First he thought it was because of the root beer float. It was like hundreds of tiny bubbles were bouncing around in there. The bubbles bounced up and down and all around. They ping-ponged their way into his chest and bing-bonged their way up into his throat. And then . . .

George let out a big burp. A *huge* burp. A SUPER burp!

The super burp was loud, and it was *magic*.

Suddenly George lost control of his

arms and legs. It was like they had minds of their own. His hands grabbed straws and stuck them up his nose like a walrus. His feet jumped up on the table and started dancing the hokey pokey. Everyone at the ice cream parlor started laughing—except George's parents, who were **covered in ice cream** from the sundaes he had knocked over.

That wasn't the only time the super burp had burst its way out of George's belly. There had been plenty of **magic gas attacks** since then. And every time the burp came, trouble followed. George never knew when a burp would strike or what it would make him do. Like dive-bomb headfirst into the principal's lap during the school talent show. Or drop raw pizza dough on his head like a giant, gooey mask. Or dance around with an angry skunk—who wound up spraying George with stinky skunk junk.

George didn't want to tell anyone about the super burp. It was hard enough being the new kid in town. But being the new kid who burped like that would just be **too weird**. So George kept his burping secret to himself.

At least, he did until Alex figured it out. Alex was smart enough to notice that George only acted weird after a mega burp burst out of him. Lucky for George, Alex had promised to keep George's secret.

Still, George was worried someone else might figure it out one day. And that was why he was really glad that Louie's hard throw hadn't knocked any burps out of him. The longer the magical super burp stayed away, the better.

Quickly, George scooped up the ball. He reached over and tagged an imaginary batter at home plate.

"Good play, George," Coach Trainer told him. Then he looked out into the field. "Next time, try not to throw so wildly, Louie. Control is important."

Louie nodded at the coach. **Then he glared at George.**

George knew that look well. Louie had been glaring at him ever since he'd arrived in Beaver Brook. George wasn't sure why Louie hated him so much. But he did.

George wasn't too crazy about Louie, either. In fact, having Louie in his school was the worst thing about Beaver Brook. Well, almost. The super burp was worse than anything—even Louie.

Chapter 2

"Hey, soldier, come on in and have some chow," George's dad greeted him as he walked into the house on Saturday afternoon.

Chow sounded really good to George. He'd been so busy with his Saturday morning job at Mr. Furstman's pet shop that he'd completely forgotten to eat any of the snacks his mom had put into his backpack that morning.

"What are we having?" George asked his dad.

"Peanut butter-and-banana sandwiches," his dad answered.

George grinned. He loved peanut

butter–and–banana sandwiches. So did his dad. It was what they always ate when George's mom was working at her craft store and the guys were left on their own.

"Come on into **the mess hall**," George's dad continued.

Mess hall was army talk for the place where people eat. George hurried in and took his spot at the table. "Mmmm . . . ," he said as he took a huge bite of gooey peanut butter and banana on wheat bread.

Brrrriiinnnnggg! Just then the phone rang. George jumped up to answer it.

"Hurro?" he said into the receiver. Pieces of chewed-up bread and banana shot out of his lips.

The peanut butter stuck to the roof of his mouth.

"George?" Julianna asked. "Is that you?"

George swallowed hard. "Yeah. Sorry. My mouth was full. What's up?"

"Do you feel like going to see the Beaver Brook Beavers play tonight? I have **an extra ticket**."

George couldn't believe his ears. Beaver Brook's minor-league team was amazing. They'd only lost one of their last ten games!

"Would I?" George gasped. "You bet!"

"Awesome," Julianna continued. "My uncle gave me four tickets. Alex and Chris are coming, too. We can pick up some great pointers watching the Beavers."

"Definitely," George said. His stomach grumbled. "We can pick up some hot dogs and popcorn, too!"

"Yep!" Julianna said with a laugh. "See you tonight!"

19

"The seats are all the way at the top," Julianna said as she, Alex, Chris, and George entered the stadium. Julianna's mom had dropped them off and was going to pick them up after the game. "But they're right behind home plate. So we can see the whole field."

"And anything we *can't* see, we can catch on **the JumboTron**." George pointed to the giant screen high above the field.

"**Weirdo warning**! There's a weirdo in the ballpark!"

Suddenly George heard Louie shouting behind him. He turned around. Louie and his older brother, Sam, were sitting in box seats just two rows from the field.

"Where are you guys going?" Louie asked George and his friends.

"To our seats." Alex pointed up toward the top of the stadium.

"Oh, you're in **the nosebleed section**," Louie said with a laugh.

Nosebleed section. George pictured a bunch of people with bloody noses all sitting together and watching the game as rivers of slimy red blood flowed down onto Louie and his brother. *Cool!*

"See ya later, Louie," Julianna said as she climbed the stairs. George, Alex, and Chris followed her. Well, George and

Alex did, anyway. Chris was so busy drawing something on his sketch pad that he turned the wrong way.

Bam! Chris slammed right into a pole. **"Excuse me, ma'am,"** he said, without even bothering to look up from his drawing.

"What's with Chris?" George asked Alex.

"He's sketching some ideas for his art-show project," Alex explained.

George watched as Chris tripped going up the stairs.

"He gets this way every year before the art show," Julianna said. "The show is this Thursday. He's only going to get worse."

SECTION 4H

Chris bumped into the knee of a huge guy sitting in an aisle seat. The guy's soda spilled onto his Beaver Brook Beavers T-shirt.

"Hey, watch where you're going, kid," the guy said, looking down at the **yucky brown soda stain** that was spreading across the front of his shirt.

"Sorry," Chris mumbled as he kept drawing and walking.

George shook his head. Chris was going to get *worse*? How was that even possible?

"Yes!" Alex exclaimed a few minutes later as the kids took their seats

and waited for the game to begin. He reached under his chair and pulled up a big glob of gray-green gum. "This nosebleed section is **a gold mine** for already been chewed gum. This is the fourth piece I've found."

"Awesome," George said. "You're four pieces closer to getting into the *Schminess Book of World Records* for the world's biggest ABC gum ball." He pulled a piece of gum from his mouth and handed it to Alex. "Take this one, too. The flavor's all gone, anyway."

"Wow! Thanks," Alex said, sticking the gum onto the giant ABC gum ball he carried around in his backpack.

"Peanuts! Popcorn! Get your snacks here!"

George looked up as a guy in a red-and-white-striped jacket and Beavers baseball cap walked down the aisle with a tray of snacks. "That's what I'm talking about!" he shouted, waving his hand. "I'll have a popcorn!" The popcorn vendor raced over. He took George's money and handed him a red-and-white-striped box.

Julianna shot George a look. "Remember why we're here," she said. "We're trying to pick up pointers that will make us better players. **Don't you want to win that championship?**"

"Yeah, but no one says I can't eat popcorn while I'm watching." George tossed piece of a popcorn in the air and caught it in his mouth.

"Good one, dude," Alex complimented him.

Chris didn't say anything. He was too busy drawing to notice.

"You guys, the game is starting." Julianna pointed toward the field. "Am I the only one here who thinks winning is important?"

George shook his head. They all wanted to win. It was just that nobody thought it was as important as Julianna did.

"Wow! That was some pitch." Julianna cheered as they watched the ball go over the plate. "Did you see how the catcher jumped up to throw it back after he caught it, George? That keeps him from making any wild throws."

George didn't answer.

"Come on, George, **focus**," Julianna insisted.

George *wanted* to focus on what was happening down on the baseball field.

But that was impossible. Because right then the only thing George could focus on was what was going on down inside his belly. There were a whole lot of bubbles bouncing around in there. And that could only mean one thing. **The super burp was back.**

Bing-bong. Ping-pong. Already the bubbles were kickboxing his kidneys and spinning on his spleen. *Ping-pong. Bing-bong.*

George tried to give Alex their secret signal. Whenever George rubbed his head and patted his stomach, Alex was supposed to pull him away before the burp could make him do something stupid in front of a bunch of people.

Rub, rub. Pat, pat.

But Alex was busy looking under his seat for more ABC gum. He didn't see that George was giving him their signal.

Zing-zoom. Bing-boom. The bubbles ricocheted off George's ribs. They tap-danced on his tongue. And then . . .

BUUURP!

George let out a grand slam of a burp. It was so loud that it actually made Chris look up from his sketch pad.

"Awesome!" Chris exclaimed.

But George didn't think it was awesome. He thought it was awful.

George opened his mouth to say, "Excuse me." But that's not what came out. Instead, George's mouth started singing. *"Take me out to the ball game. Take me out with the crowd! Buy me some peanuts and Cracker Jack!"*

"Dude! No!" Alex shouted.

The next thing George knew, his legs leaped up out of his seat. His feet ran over to the guy selling snacks. His hands grabbed some of the boxes.

"Peanuts, popcorn, Cracker Jack!" George's mouth shouted out.

"Hey, that's *my* job!" the vendor shouted. "Give me back those snacks!"

George wanted to give the guy back his snacks. He wanted his feet to walk back to his seat, and he wanted his rear end to sit down. The only trouble was George wasn't in charge anymore. The super burp was.

"Let me root, root, root for the home team!" George's mouth sang out. His feet danced up and down the aisles. His hands juggled boxes of peanuts, popcorn, and Cracker Jack.

Unfortunately, George wasn't a very good juggler. **Boxes of snacks went flying all over the place.** The snack vendor ran around trying to catch them.

A stadium guard raced to the nosebleed section. "Cut it out, kid!" he shouted. "Sit down. And give back those snacks."

But the
super burp didn't
want to give back any
snacks. And it sure didn't
want to sit down.
**Burps aren't very
good sitters.**
The guard
grabbed for George.
George darted out
of the way. The
guard fell into the lap
of a woman in
a Beavers
baseball cap.
"What are
you doing?!" the woman
demanded.
"Somebody catch that kid!" the
guard shouted.
"If they don't win, it's a shame,"

George sang out. By now the whole stadium was singing with him. *"For it's one . . . two . . . three strikes . . ."*

"Check it out! **George is on the JumboTron!**" Chris cheered. He pointed to the giant screen.

Pop! Just then, George felt the air rush right out of him. It was like someone had popped a balloon in his belly. The super burp was gone! But George was still there, in the middle of the stadium, surrounded by boxes of snacks.

And it was all up there on the JumboTron for everyone to see.

The guard glared at George. "Well, kid?" he asked. "What do you have to say for yourself?"

George opened his mouth to say, **"I'm sorry."** And that's exactly what came out.

The guard grabbed George by the arm and started pulling him out of the stadium. "I'm calling your parents to pick you up. You're out of here," he said.

George figured that was what was going to happen. It was the same thing every time. The burp had all the fun, and George got in all the trouble. *Bubble* trouble. The worst kind there was.

BUS STOP

THIS MEANS YOU, KID!

STAY OFF MY LAWN!

34

Chapter 3

"I'm really sorry I didn't leave with you Saturday night," Alex told George when the boys walked to school together on Monday morning. "I tried to, but Julianna made me stay and take notes on the plays the Beavers were making. She's **obsessed** with winning this game."

"It's okay," George said. "My mom came and got me. She was really, really mad. It's probably better you weren't in the car with us."

"If it makes you feel any better, Louie was **superjealous** you got to be on the JumboTron and he didn't," Alex told him. "We ran into him after the game, and he was still mad about it. I'm telling you, dude. His face was so red, I thought it was going to explode."

George grinned, imagining Louie's head exploding like a giant volcano.

"That was definitely one of your biggest burps yet," Alex said.

George frowned. "Yeah, I think they're getting worse."

"Well, I went on The Burp No More Blog, and I think I have a new idea for stopping the burps," Alex told him. "You gotta **stop chewing gum**. Because the more you chew, the more you let air into your stomach. And the more air . . ."

"The more gas," George said, finishing his thought. "And the more burps. It makes sense. Only . . ."

"Only what?" Alex asked.

"If I stop chewing gum, I can't help you build up your record-breaking ABC gum ball," George explained.

"Sure you can," Alex said. "You don't have to chew it yourself. You can help me find ABC gum under chairs and tables or on park benches. It's everywhere."

George thought about that for a minute. "Yeah, I guess," he said finally. "I can stop chewing gum if I have to."

"Sure you can," Alex told him. "It will totally be worth it."

George smiled. **"You're not kidding."**

"Hot lunch today will be tuna surprise." A fifth-grader named Sasha read from her note cards during the morning announcements on the school's television station, WEBS TV. "And our art teacher, Mrs. Jasper, is keeping the art room open after school every day this week for students who want to work on their projects for Thursday's art show."

George yawned and then chewed off a piece of his fingernail. He had thought having a school TV station was going to be really exciting. But now he realized that nothing ever happened at Edith B. Sugarman Elementary School. And that meant there was **never anything exciting** to announce.

"And now we'll hear from Julianna with her sports update," Sasha said.

George stopped chewing his nail and tried to pay attention. After all, Julianna was his friend.

"This Friday, the Edith B. Sugarman Elementary Sea Monkeys will be battling it out against the undefeated Klockermeister Elementary Kangaroos for the fourth-grade baseball championship," Julianna said. "Come cheer on the Sea Monkeys as we prepare to take back the trophy!"

"Sea Monkeys! Sea Monkeys! Sea Monkeys!" George cheered. He couldn't help himself.

Suddenly George's teacher, Mrs. Kelly, stood up. *Uh-oh.* This couldn't be good.

"You're gonna get it now," Louie whispered to him.

George gulped.

Mrs. Kelly walked over to George's desk. She stood right over him, glaring. And then a huge smile broke out on her face.

"Sea Monkeys! Sea Monkeys! Sea

Monkeys!" Mrs. Kelly cheered.

"Sea Monkeys! Sea Monkeys! Sea Monkeys!" the class cheered back.

They were still cheering when Julianna walked into the classroom a few minutes later and took her seat in the front of the room.

Mrs. Kelly smiled. "Now that I have all my sea monkeys in place, it's time to start our science unit." She reached down under her desk and pulled out a plastic aquarium.

George had seen aquariums like that at Mr. Furstman's pet shop. They were usually filled with pretty fish. But there weren't any guppies, bettas, or angelfish swimming in this tank. All George could see were **tiny, creepy creatures** in the water. They had long sticklike bodies and two huge black circles at the tops of the sticks that kind of looked like eyeballs.

"What are those things?" Sage asked. She made a face. "They look **nasty**."

Mrs. Kelly smiled at her. "Those," she said, "are sea monkeys."

The kids all stared at their teacher in surprise.

"They can't be sea monkeys," Louie said. "They don't have any arms. And they aren't eating bananas or saying *ook, ook, ook*."

"Sorry, Louie, but *sea* monkeys don't act like *zoo* monkeys," Mrs. Kelly explained. "Because sea monkeys aren't monkeys at all. They're **brine shrimp**."

George couldn't believe his ears. "You mean we're actually the Edith B. Sugarman Elementary *Shrimp*?" he asked.

Mrs. Kelly laughed. "I guess so," she said.

"So why do they call them monkeys?" Alex asked.

Mrs. Kelly shrugged. "I guess because they look like they're playing around while they swim. And because they have tails."

"They do look like they're having fun in there," George admitted.

"That's what you do on the baseball field," Mrs. Kelly said. "Have fun."

"And we win," Julianna added.

"Don't forget about winning."

"How can we? You won't let us," Louie told her.

"Winning is fun," Mrs. Kelly agreed. "But it isn't everything, Julianna."

Julianna didn't argue. But she didn't look convinced, either.

"I thought it would be fun to learn about sea monkeys this week," Mrs. Kelly told the class. "After all, they're who we are. We should be proud of them."

Proud? George groaned. Who could *ever* be proud of being called **a teeny-weeny sea shrimp**?

Chapter 4

"I'm telling you, guys," George said as he and his friends sat down at the lunch table later that afternoon. "If the Klockermeister Kangaroos ever find out what sea monkeys really are, they'll never let us live it down. They'll call us shrimp. We'll be **the laughingstock** of the whole league."

"Not if we destroy the Kangaroos on the field," Julianna insisted. "Then the only thing we'll be called is champions."

"But no one can beat those guys," Alex pointed out. "They're amazing . . . and undefeated."

"We can beat them," Julianna said.

"We're just going to have to work hard. I say we have **an extra practice** at recess."

"Good idea," Alex agreed.

"Definitely," George added.

"You *need* extra practice, George," Louie told him as he walked by. "Practice in how not to be weird!"

Max and Mike started laughing.

"Good one," Max told Louie.

"Your best one yet," Mike added.

George rolled his eyes. If that was the best Louie had, George had nothing to worry about—other than the super burp making him do more weird things, anyway.

"I have some new pitches I want to work on," Julianna told George. "You and I will have to come up with some more signals."

"I want to practice bunting," Alex said.

Everyone was getting very excited

about the idea of an extra baseball practice at recess. Well, *almost* everyone.

Chris shook his head. "I'm not going to be able to practice at recess today," he said.

"What are you talking about?" George asked him. "We're all practicing."

"I can't," Chris insisted. "I have to go to the art room and work on my project. The art show is only three days away."

"And the game's only four days away," George told him. **"Which one's more important?"**

Chris shrugged. "The art show. I really want to win that blue ribbon for the best piece in the show."

George's eyes nearly bugged out of his head.

"I told you. He always gets obsessed before the art show," Julianna told George.

"You don't have a chance at winning that blue ribbon," Louie told Chris. "My dad has hired a really famous artist to help me with my project. His name is **Pablo Zoocaso**."

George didn't think it was fair for Louie to have a real artist helping him with his project. But that wasn't the point right now.

"I didn't know the season was going to go on this long," Chris explained. "If I thought we were going to make it all the way to the championship, I wouldn't have joined the team."

"You only joined the team because you thought we would be losers?" George asked, surprised.

"I joined because I wanted to hang out with you guys," Chris answered.

"We're not hanging out. We're *winning!*" Julianna insisted.

Chris's face was turning red. "No matter how much we practice, we can't beat the Kangaroos!" he shouted. "We're just a bunch of **wimpy shrimpies!**"

Wow! George had never seen Chris get upset like this before. Julianna wasn't kidding when she said Chris got crazy right before the art show. He was acting just plain nuts!

"I can't believe Chris didn't come to practice after school, either," George said as he and Alex headed home late that afternoon.

"Coach gave him the afternoon off to work with Mrs. Jasper," Alex reminded him.

"I know the art show's important," George said, "but what about **team loyalty**?"

"He'll be at the next practice," Alex assured George.

Just then, two kids in Klockermeister Kangaroos T-shirts walked up to Alex and George.

"Look, it's a couple of Sea Monkeys," one of the Kangaroos said.

"We're gonna **destroy** you guys," the second Kangaroo said.

"Oh yeah?" George asked. "What makes you so sure?"

"Because sea monkeys are just *wimpy shrimpies*," the first Kangaroo told him. "Kangaroos can stomp them out with one hop." He stomped his foot, **smashing an imaginary sea monkey** into the sidewalk. Then the two Kangaroos ran off laughing.

"Did you hear that?" George asked Alex. "Those are **the exact words** Chris used. He's probably so angry from lunch that he told the Kangaroos who we really are."

"You don't know that. Anyone could come up with that rhyme," Alex said. But he looked upset. "Chris would never tell anyone that sea monkeys are shrimp," he continued. "It's not like him."

George shook his head. It wasn't like Chris to yell at everyone in the middle of the cafeteria, either. Alex could believe what he wanted. But George knew better. "We're the laughingstock of the whole league," George groaned. "And it's all Chris's fault! Chris is a **TRAITOR!**"

Chapter 5

"I did not tell anyone that we were brine shrimp or wimpy shrimpies!" Chris said the next morning when the team gathered on the playground before school.

"Come on, **admit it**," George insisted. He turned to the other kids. "They called us wimpy shrimpies—the exact words that Chris used. You should have heard those Kangaroos laughing," he added.

"They're using this to **psych us out**," Julianna said with a frown. "It's gonna give them a big advantage. Chris, you really messed things up for us."

"I can't believe you guys think I would do something like that," Chris shot back.

"It sure seems like you did," Louie told him. "We were all at practice, so we couldn't have been the ones who told them. But we don't know where *you* were yesterday afternoon."

"I was in the art room," Chris said.

"So you say," Louie told him.

Chris looked at Alex. "You believe me, don't you?" he asked.

Alex shrugged. "I don't know what to believe," he said honestly.

"You guys are being **jerks**," Chris said.

"*We're* jerks?" George said. "*You're* the traitor."

Chris glared at George. George glared back at Chris.

"If that's what you think, I don't want to be on your stupid old team, anyway," Chris told them. **"I quit!"** He turned and stormed off.

"You can't quit!" George shouted back. "We fire you."

Chris kept walking.

"It doesn't matter if he quits or we fire him," Julianna said. "We're still in trouble. We don't have a left fielder anymore. What are we gonna do?"

"We could ask Charlie to play," Alex suggested.

"Or Abby G.," Mike tried. "She could use her older brother's glove."

"*I'll* take Chris's place," Sage piped up suddenly.

George's head whipped around.

He hadn't even noticed that Sage was there.

"You don't know anything about baseball," Julianna told Sage.

"That's okay." Sage flashed George a big smile and batted her eyelashes. "Georgie can teach me everything he knows. We can even have special extra practices together. Just Georgie and me."

George groaned. There was *no* way *that* was happening.

"We do need a left fielder," Alex said slowly.

"And it doesn't matter if she can catch or not because *I'm* on third base," Louie reminded everyone. "That's right in front of left field. I'll catch those balls before they ever get near Sage."

"Isn't this great, Georgie?" **Sage cooed.** "We're teammates now."

No. It *wasn't* great. It stunk. Baseball practice had been one of the few places, where George could get away from Sage's goofy smiles and creepy batting eyelashes. But now she was going to be *everywhere* he was. *Oh, brother.*

"Georgie, wait up!" Sage called out to George after school that day. "We're going to the same place. We can walk to the field together."

George did *not* wait up. Instead he walked faster toward the baseball field. He was in a rotten mood. It was bad enough that he'd had to spend all of recess with Sage making **googly eyes** at him on the baseball field, but now he had to spend his *after*-school time with her, too. And **it was all Chris's fault**.

"Hey, dude," Alex said as George met up with him on the baseball field. "Check it out! I've found three more pieces of gum under the bench in the visitors' dugout."

"Awesome," George said. "I still wish I could chew gum for your gum ball."

"Don't worry about it," Alex said. He put his gum ball into his backpack for safekeeping. "There's plenty of ABC gum in the world. Besides, it's for your own good. You haven't had any more burp attacks, have you?"

George shook his head. "**Not one.** That's pretty much the only thing that's gone right lately. I mean, first I find out I'm on the Brine Shrimp baseball team. Then Chris quits. And now . . ."

"Georgie, didn't you hear me calling you?" Sage asked as she arrived at the field.

"And now *that*," George said, rolling

his eyes at Sage.

"Okay, team!" Coach Trainer said. "It's **practice time**. Sage, you should probably hit first, since you haven't had as much practice as the other kids have had. The rest of you, take your positions on the field."

George pulled down his catcher's mask and crouched behind Sage at home plate. He put down four fingers. That was the signal for a curveball.

Julianna nodded and threw the ball. It soared right past home plate. It was a perfect pitch. But Sage didn't even swing.

"How come you didn't swing?" Julianna asked her. "You could have hit that."

"I was afraid I might hit the catcher with the bat," Sage said. "I don't want to hurt Georgie."

All the kids laughed. Louie laughed

the loudest. "I love when she calls him Georgie," he said.

"You should talk, Loo Loo Poo!" George barked back at him.

"Come on, kids. Cool it," Coach Trainer reminded George and Louie. He turned to Sage. "You can swing as hard as you want," he told her. "Georgie . . . I mean *George* . . . will be fine."

"He called him Georgie!" Louie started laughing all over again.

Grrrr . . . George could feel his face turning **beet red** and hot—so hot that he was sure big blasts of steam were erupting from his ears.

If Chris had been up to bat, none of this would be happening. But now that Chris had quit and Sage had taken his place, baseball practice was just **one big embarrassment**.

He was never going to forgive Chris for this. NEVER!

Sage struck out really quickly. Unfortunately, Louie went up to bat next. *He* wasn't worried about hurting George. In fact, he probably wanted to.

"You better not mess up the game," Louie hissed in his direction. "When my big brother, Sam, went to this school, they won the championship. He has a trophy for it and everything. I want a trophy, too."

George frowned. Did Louie think he was the only one who wanted a trophy? He reached his hand down and gave Julianna the signal for a fastball. It was her best pitch.

Zoom! Julianna pitched the ball. It flew across the field so fast, Louie barely saw it.

"Hey! No fair!" Louie said. "That one was **too fast**."

"That's why it's called a fastball," Julianna answered.

George laughed and crouched back down. He gave Julianna the signal for a curveball. She nodded and let the pitch fly.

Crack! This time Louie managed to hit the ball. Only it didn't fly into the field. Instead the ball popped up backward. George reached up his glove and caught it in midair.

"Yer out!" he shouted.

Louie glared at him. "You did that on purpose!" he shouted at George.

Duh. "That's my job," George said. "I catch the ball. I'm the catcher, remember?"

"But how am I supposed to practice

my running if you catch my pop foul?"
Louie demanded.

It was **a ridiculous argument**. And
George would have told Louie so—if
he wasn't suddenly afraid to open his
mouth. Not because of what Louie might
say or do, but because of what the *super
burp* might do. Suddenly that burp
was bing-bonging and ping-ponging in
George's belly. If it slipped out, who knew
what would happen?

The burp was moving fast! It had
already cling-clanged over George's colon
and was now bouncing on his bladder.
George had to get out of there before the
burp burst and made him do something
totally goofy!

He quickly gave Alex the signal. He
patted his head and rubbed his belly.

Whoosh! Julianna sent a fast, curving
pitch soaring toward the plate.

"Julianna!" Coach Trainer shouted. "Who are you pitching to? There's no batter at the plate."

"But George just gave me **the knuckleball-forkball-changeup signal**," Julianna said.

George hadn't been asking for a pitch. He'd been asking for help. But Alex must have thought George was giving Julianna baseball signals, too.

Now the burp was hip-hopping on George's heart. He *had* to get Alex's attention. He rubbed his belly and patted his head again.

"See, now George's giving me the signal for . . . for . . ." Julianna paused. "I have no idea," she said.

But Alex recognized the signal— finally. "Dude, not again!" he shouted as he ran toward George.

Oh yeah. Again. *Bing-bong. Ping-pong.*

The super burp was really strong. But George was stronger. If he could just get those bubbles to slide back down to his feet . . .

SLIDE! That was it! George took a running leap and did **a belly flop**. Then he slid face-first toward third base.

Pop! Suddenly George felt something burst inside. The air rushed right out of him. The super burp was gone.

Coach Trainer came running over. "Good try, George," he said. "But you're supposed to hit the ball before you slide."

George opened his mouth to spit out a glob of dirt and grass, and that's exactly what happened. "Blech," George said as the mound of **brownish-green grime** shot out of him.

"George ate dirt!" Louie laughed. "He's such a weirdo freak!"

"The weirdo-est," Max agreed.

"The freakiest," Mike added.

The three of them laughed. But George didn't care. He had squelched the belch! And nothing else mattered.

Chapter 6

"The not-chewing-gum burp cure isn't working," George said later that afternoon as he and Alex walked home together from practice. "You saw what happened out there. If I hadn't taken that slide, the burp would've **blasted right out** of me."

"But it didn't," Alex pointed out. "There have been plenty of times when you *couldn't* stop the burps. There was something different about this one." Alex sounded very serious, like **a real scientist**. "This burp was weak enough for you to stop. Maybe it was less powerful because you haven't been chewing gum. Without the gum, you've stopped feeding your burps any extra gas."

George didn't argue. It was tough to argue with someone as smart and logical as Alex. Besides, maybe he was right.

It sure *seemed* like Alex had found a cure for the not-so-common burp. By the time Thursday morning rolled around, George realized that he had not burped at all. George didn't miss the burp one bit. What he did miss was Chris. Not that he was forgiving him or anything.

Still, George was **going crazy** wondering what kind of art project could be so important that it would make Chris quit the baseball team and turn into a traitor. He just had to know. So George did something he had never, ever done before.

He got to school early! And he went

inside before the bell even rang. He had to. It was the only way he could sneak into the auditorium with no one else around. That was where the art show was set up.

Each piece of artwork in the auditorium was covered with a cloth to keep it from getting dirty. And in front of each piece was a card with the name of the artist. George found Chris's piece in the back of the room. He whipped off the cloth and . . . *WOW!* George couldn't believe his eyes. He was standing face-to-face with a **humongous, clay sea monkey!**

The sea monkey was amazing. It had big, bulging muscles in its tail and chest. Its eyes were black and piercing. Instead of being a wimpy shrimpy, *this* sea monkey was **strong and powerful**. A sign at the bottom of the sculpture read SUGARMAN SEA MONKEYS MASCOT.

Wow. Now George knew for sure that Chris hadn't spoken to the Kangaroos. There was no way the kid who built this could ever have been a traitor to the Sea Monkeys. Alex had been right: The Kangaroos *must* have learned the truth about sea monkeys on their own. And they had probably made up the rhyme themselves, too. After all, how hard was it to come up with one?

Suddenly George felt bad about how he had treated Chris. It wasn't fair of him to try to force Chris to play baseball when he loved art so much. And he was really wrong to call him a traitor.

The worst part was, George couldn't even apologize—without letting Chris know he'd sneaked a peek at his secret sculpture. And that would just make everything worse.

"I think we have everything ready . . ."

Uh-oh! George heard Mrs. Jasper's voice. It sounded like she was coming down the hallway and heading toward the auditorium. He had to get out of there. Quickly George threw the cloth back over Chris's sea-monkey sculpture. He turned toward the door and . . . *craacckkk!*

Uh-oh . . . *again.* As George turned around a piece of the sea monkey's clay tail fell to the floor. **George had broken Chris's sculpture!** The sculpture his friend had spent a whole week creating. The sculpture that could have won him a blue ribbon.

Worse yet, when Chris found out that it was George who had broken the sculpture, their friendship would be broken forever. Chris would never believe that it had been an accident. Not with the way George had been acting.

Oh man. This was *ba-a-ad*! George had to fix the sculpture before the art show. Somehow he had to stick that piece of tail back on the sea monkey. But what could he find that would be **sticky enough** to glue it back on? He doubted the paste he had in his desk was strong enough to glue clay. George was going to need something really sticky to get him out of this sticky situation. Sticky . . . like *gum*.

Only George wasn't chewing gum anymore. But he knew someone who had lots of gum. And it was already chewed, all soft and sticky. All George had to do was swipe a few pieces of fresh ABC gum off the gum ball sitting in Alex's backpack and use them to fix the sculpture. It was **the perfect plan**.

Except if George took gum off Alex's gum ball, then Alex would be further from his goal of breaking the world record.

But George didn't have time to think about that now. Mrs. Jasper's footsteps were getting closer. Quickly he shoved the piece of sea monkey tail in his pocket and raced out of the auditorium.

George waited all morning for the chance to sneak some gum from Alex's ABC gum ball. Finally, when it was lunchtime, he got his chance. While the other kids went to the cafeteria, George snuck back into the classroom. He dug into Alex's backpack and found the ABC gum ball. It was wrapped in a huge plastic bag to keep it from sticking to Alex's papers.

George **yanked a big hunk** of gray gum from the top layer of the ball. The pieces of gum were still soft and gooey—they'd probably just been chewed when Alex had gotten his hands on them. *Yes!* That made them perfect for sticking.

Quickly George put the gum ball back in Alex's bag and then raced out of the classroom as fast as he could. He had to get that piece stuck back onto the sea monkey before anyone noticed that it was missing.

Unfortunately, Principal McKeon was just around the corner.

"George, where are you supposed to be?" Mrs. McKeon asked, stopping George in his tracks.

"I . . . um . . . I was going to the bathroom before lunch," George fibbed. "But I'm all done now."

"Oh, okay," Mrs. McKeon said. "Well, hurry up and meet your class."

"Yes, ma'am," George said. He raced off. *Phew*. That had been **a close one**.

A few minutes later, George was back in the auditorium. He knew he didn't have much time. Any minute now, Mrs. Jasper or one of the other teachers might stop by.

George placed a few pieces of gum on the butt of the mascot, right where the tail needed to be. He shoved the clay tail back on and held it for a minute to make sure it stuck. Then he stepped back to admire his work.

Not bad. You couldn't even see the crack unless you went up really, really close. And who was going to get that close to **a sea monkey's butt**?

George was feeling pretty good about himself as he left the auditorium. He was a good friend after all. **He'd just saved Chris's butt.** Well, actually he'd saved Chris's *sea monkey's* butt. But it was pretty much the same thing.

Now all he had to do was find a few pieces of ABC gum to replace the ones he'd taken from Alex. That shouldn't be hard. Kids were always sticking gum where it didn't belong. All George had to do was look behind one of the toilets in the boys' bathroom or under the bleachers in the gym.

Rumble. Grumble.

Just then, George felt something weird deep in his belly.

Grrrrr. Rrrrr.

Those noises could only mean one thing: *George was hungry.*

Rumble. Grumble. Grrrrr. Rrrrr.

Really, *really* hungry.

But George's stomach was going to have to wait. He still had one more stop to make before he ate lunch—the bathroom, to wash his hands. Because there was no way George was touching his food while he had sea monkey–butt clay and ABC gum spit on his hands. That would just be *way* too gross.

83

ART
SHOW

SCULPTURE
OF
MOM
BY MAX

Chapter 7

"We're finally going to get to see what Chris has been working on," Alex said that night, as he and George walked into the auditorium for the art show.

George already knew all about Chris's sculpture. But of course he didn't say that. He didn't say anything. He was **too worried**. Worried that the gum wasn't sticky enough and the tail on the sculpture had broken off again. Worried that Alex would figure out that someone had swiped a big glob of ABC gum from his gum ball. Worried that Chris was still mad about quitting the baseball team. Worried . . .

"Georgie! There you are!" Sage cried out.

. . . Worried that Sage would be following him all around the art show.

"I knew you'd be one of the first people here," Sage said as she raced to George's side. "That's why I made my parents hurry to the school. I didn't want to lose you in the crowd."

George glanced toward the table of refreshments. Sage's parents were standing there talking to Alex's and George's parents. They were all sipping cups of coffee and snacking on cookies and doughnuts. With all the grown-ups around, **George couldn't totally ignore Sage**. He had to be at least a little nice to her.

"Yeah, well, we wanted to see Chris's artwork," George said.

"We're really curious," Alex added.

Just then, Julianna came running over. "Hi, guys!" she said. "You didn't go over to see Chris's piece without me, did you?"

George shook his head. "We just got here."

"Great," Julianna said. She looked around the room. "There he is," she said, pointing to where Chris was standing.

The kids all headed over toward Chris. But before they got very far, they came face-to-face with a huge painting of a . . . well . . . um . . . a . . . George wasn't sure *what* it was!

"What is that?" Julianna asked.

"I'm not sure," Alex said. "Is that a big toe in the top corner?"

"I thought it was a thumb," Sage said.

"Why is there a pineapple in the middle of that cat face?" George wondered.

"That's not a pineapple," Alex said. "I'm pretty sure it's a basketball."

"And that's not a cat," Sage added. "It's a lollipop with hair on it."

"You think Mrs. Jasper hung it upside down by mistake?" George suggested.

Julianna bent over and tipped her head, so she could look at it upside down. "No," she said. "It still doesn't make any sense."

Just then Louie, Max, and Mike walked over.

"So you like my painting, huh?" Louie said. "I'm not surprised. Pablo Zoocaso said I have **real talent**."

George wondered how much Mr. Farley had to pay Pablo Zoocaso to tell Louie that.

"Um . . . what do you call this?" George asked Louie.

"*Self-Portrait*," Louie said. "Can't you tell?"

"*This* is a picture of *you*?" Alex asked.

"It really looks like you, Louie," Mike said. "Especially that eye on the bottom left."

"That's not an eye," Louie barked at him. "That's **a banana with a brown spot** in the middle. Bananas are my favorite food."

"I thought that was your nose," Max said. "With a pimple on it."

Louie frowned. "I should have known that you guys weren't smart enough to appreciate great modern art."

"It's great," Mike assured him.

"And modern," Max added. "The modernest."

"I'm going to go over and see what Chris made," Julianna said. She turned to George, Alex, and Sage. "You guys coming?"

George still hadn't made up with

Chris. But he didn't really want to be enemies with him forever. And he definitely didn't want to stand there looking at Louie's weird painting anymore.

"I'm coming," George said.

"Me too," Alex added.

"Me too, Georgie," Sage agreed.

George rolled his eyes.

"Well, tell him I'm sorry he won't get that blue ribbon," Louie said. "My painting is **going to win** for the best artwork in the show. Mrs. Jasper is definitely going to recognize my talent."

Only if she can figure out that a pineapple might be a basketball and what looks like an eye could be a banana with a pimple, George thought.

"Wow!" Alex exclaimed as he and the other kids finally saw Chris's sculpture.

"That's the best art project you've ever done."

"It's the greatest sea monkey I've ever seen," George told Chris.

"Thanks, George." A big smile formed on Chris's face.

"Now I know why you needed so much time in the art room," George said.

"I probably shouldn't have joined the baseball team in the first place," Chris admitted.

"That's okay," Sage said. She moved closer to George. "It all worked out perfectly."

George stepped away from her.

"I bet you'll win the blue ribbon with this," Julianna said, looking at the clay sea monkey.

"Maybe," Chris said. "But the important thing is that it turned out exactly the way I pictured it."

"Have the judges been by yet?" Alex asked him.

Chris nodded. "Mrs. Jasper and Principal McKeon are the judges. They walked around the whole art show this afternoon before anyone got here."

Chris was **totally cool**. He didn't seem to have a single nervous butterfly in his belly. But *George* had something in his. *Something big, bubbly, and dangerous.* Something that bing-bonged and ping-ponged. The super burp was back!

Already the bubbles were cling-clanging on his colon and bing-banging around his large intestine. Bubble, bubble. George was in trouble!

George turned to Alex. He rubbed his head and patted his belly. He patted his head and rubbed his belly.

"Dude, no!" Alex shouted.

Dude, yes! The bubbles were forcing

their way up into George's throat. They were undulating on his uvula and using his tongue as a trampoline.

Alex grabbed George's arm and started to pull him out of the auditorium.

Alex was too late. George let out a burp so loud that everyone in the room stopped talking. They all **turned and stared** at George.

George opened his mouth to say, "Excuse me." But that's not what came out. Instead he shouted, "IT'S ARTY-PARTY TIME!"

"Let's get out of here," Alex whispered.

But the burp had no intention of leaving. It wanted to be part of the art show!

The next thing George knew, his

feet were dancing up and down the
aisles of the art show. They stopped
at a sculpture of a cat. Now the rest of
George's body wanted in on the fun. He
got down on all fours. Then his back
arched up like an angry cat.

"Hiss!" George's mouth shouted.

"George, get up from the floor!" his
mother shouted.

"Meow!" George's mouth answered
her. He didn't get up. Instead he started
crawling around the room like a cat
stalking a mouse.

"George, you heard your mother!" George's father bellowed. "Get on your feet, soldier!"

Surprisingly, George *did* stand up. He ran over to the refreshments table. "Jelly doughnuts!" he shouted.

George's hands reached out and grabbed four doughnuts. Then his feet ran over to the wall of the auditorium. His hands squeezed the doughnuts—hard. Streams of red jelly squirted out of the doughnuts and onto the wall.

"Finger paints!" George shouted. His fingers began sloshing around in the jelly.

"George Brown, stop that this instant!" Principal McKeon shouted angrily.

George wanted to stop. He really did. But George wasn't in charge anymore. The super burp was. And it wanted to paint. His fingers swirled faster and faster, making a jelly finger painting on the wall.

"More jelly!" George shouted.

"Just what do you think you're doing?" Mrs. Jasper demanded.

"Finger painting!" George shouted back. "Arty-party time! Ha-ha-ha-ha-ha!" George's fingers swirled and swirled. He laughed harder and harder. The grown-ups got more and more angry. And then . . .

Pop! Suddenly George felt the air rush right out of him. The super burp was gone. But George was still there. And so was the giant jelly-doughnut finger painting on the wall.

George opened his mouth to say, "I'm sorry." And that's exactly what came out.

His mother looked at him. "Sometimes I don't know **what gets into you,** George," she said.

George didn't answer. What could he say? It wasn't what got into him that got him into trouble. It was what slipped *out* of him. That rotten, horrible, stupid super burp.

Chapter 8

"That was a bum deal," Alex said after school the next day as he and George walked over to the baseball field. "Having to clean up the whole auditorium after the art show must have taken you hours."

"It did," George told him. "While you guys were out having ice cream to celebrate Chris winning the blue ribbon, I was cleaning jelly off the walls. But it was **either clean up or get grounded**. And no way was I missing the championship game today."

George popped three big pieces of gum into his mouth and started chewing.

He held the pack up to Alex. "You want a piece?" he asked him.

"Sure," Alex said. "I need it. My ball actually shrank overnight. But I can't think of **any scientific reason** for it."

George looked at the ground. He knew why the gum ball had shrunk. And he felt rotten about it.

"Are you sure *you* should be chewing gum, though?"

Of course George was sure. He had to replace the glob of gum he'd taken from Alex's ABC gum ball the day before. But he didn't say that. Instead he said, "I burped really badly last night, even though I wasn't chewing. So that's not a cure."

"I guess," Alex said. "But don't give up. I'll figure out a cure eventually."

George frowned. *Eventually* sounded very, very far away.

Just then Chris came running to catch up to his pals. "Hey, guys!" he said.

"What are you doing here?" George asked.

"I may not be on the team, but I'm still going to cheer you on," Chris said. "Like you guys did for me last night."

"You should have seen Louie's face when they gave you the blue ribbon," George said with a smile. "He took it pretty poorly when his painting didn't win."

"I heard him say that his dad should sue Pablo Zoocaso." Alex laughed.

"They're going to put the sculpture in the front of the school—**right next to your championship trophy**," Chris said happily.

George frowned. He wished he were as confident about winning that trophy as Chris was. The Sea Monkeys were a good team. But so were the Kangaroos. And the Kangaroos didn't have a catcher with a magic super burp that messed things up all the time. The burp was an extra player George—and the other Sea Monkeys— could definitely do without!

"Yoo-hoo! Georgie!" Sage called as she ran toward the field.

George groaned. Sage was something else the Sea Monkeys could do without.

"We better hurry up," Alex said. "The Klockermeister Kangaroos' bus just showed up. The game's starting any minute."

George picked up the pace. "Go Sea Monkeys!" he chanted. "Go Sea Monkeys! GO! GO! GO!"

George looked at Julianna and then dropped his closed fist toward the ground. It was the signal for a slider.

Julianna shook her head no.

George thought for a second. This was an important pitch. The batter already had two strikes against him. And the Kangaroos had two outs, with a player on third. If Julianna could just strike this guy out, the Sea Monkeys would be up to bat.

Finally George dropped one finger. Fastball.

Julianna nodded and **let it rip**.

Whoosh! The pitch flew toward the plate at top speed.

Crack! The Kangaroo at the plate slammed the ball toward left field.

"I got it! I got it!" Sage shouted. She ran for the ball.

"I got it! I got it!" Louie shouted. He ran for the ball.

Crash! Louie and Sage **banged** right into each other.

Plop! The baseball fell to the ground between them.

The batter raced toward first base. The runner on third base headed for home. Louie scrambled for the ball. He picked it up and threw it toward George. The throw was high and **out of control**. George jumped up and reached his glove toward the sky. He caught the ball just as the runner crossed home plate.

"SAFE!" the umpire shouted.

George looked up at the scoreboard: **4–3**. The Kangaroos were in the lead.

"George! Why didn't you tag him out?" Louie demanded.

Why? *WHY?* Maybe because Louie had thrown the ball so crazily, he could barely catch it. Or maybe because Sage and Louie had taken way too long figuring out which one of them should pick up the ball and throw it to him.

Just then a roar went through the crowd. Everyone started cheering.

George turned around to see Mrs. Kelly dancing on top of the Sea Monkeys' dugout. She was wearing a cheerleading uniform with a big *S* on the front.

"Let's go Sea Monkeys! Let's go!" Mrs. Kelly shouted. She shook her pom-poms and **wiggled her rear end**.

George groaned. There were some things a guy should never have to see—and his teacher wiggling in a cheerleading uniform was one of them.

The home team fans clapped louder. "Sea Monkeys! Sea Monkeys!"

The sound of the clapping and cheering made George smile. He was **more determined than ever to win** this game. The Kangaroos were only ahead by one run. There were still two innings to go. This game wasn't over yet.

"Batter up!" the umpire called out.

The Kangaroo batter came to the plate. George dropped four fingers toward the ground. Curveball.

Julianna nodded and let the pitch fly.

The batter waited for it to come near the bat. Then he swung. *Crack!* The ball flew up in the air—backward! George jumped back, reached up his glove, and caught the ball in midair.

"*Yer* out!" the umpire shouted.

"Woo-hoo!" Alex cheered.

"Good catch, Georgie," Sage called to him.

"George! George! George!" the crowd cheered. Mrs. Kelly did a somersault in front of the bleachers. By now the only one not cheering for him was Louie. Even Max and Mike were cheering—at least until Louie told them to stop.

George grinned. Take *that*, Kangaroos!

George looked over at Mrs. Kelly. She was **trying** to do a cartwheel. She held out her arms, flipped over to the side, and—*bam!*—landed right on her rear end.

"Okay, Louie, you're up," Coach Trainer said.

Louie headed to the plate. He swung the bat over his shoulder and waited for the pitch.

"Louie! Louie!" the Sea Monkeys shouted.

"Louie's gonna go kablooie!" Mike cheered.

George was the only one on the team who wasn't cheering. But not because he hated Louie—which he did. George wasn't cheering because there was something else that was **gonna go kablooie** any minute now. Something that bing-bonged and cling-clonged. Something that could cause a whole lot of trouble. The super burp was back!

George shut his mouth tight, trying to keep the burp from escaping. He rubbed his belly and patted his head, trying to give Alex their signal. But Alex was too busy watching the game to notice.

The super burp was on the move. It wasn't even stopping to kickbox George's kidneys or rap on his ribs. It just shot right up George's throat, into his mouth, and . . .

B-U-U-U-R-P!

George let out a burp that was so loud and so strong, it blew right over the center-field wall—**a home run of a super burp!**

"Dude, no!" Alex cried out.

Dude, yes! The super burp was out and ready to play. The next thing George knew, his legs were running out of the dugout, and his hands were waving in the air.

"George! Get back here!" Coach Trainer yelled.

George wanted to go back to the dugout. He really did. But George wasn't in charge anymore. The super burp was. And it wanted to cheer with Mrs. Kelly! George grabbed his teacher by the elbow and swung her around.

The crowd cheered. But Louie didn't. He was so busy watching George, he missed a great pitch.

"Strike!" the umpire shouted.

"George! Cut it out!" Louie shouted. "I can't bat while you're acting weird!"

But George wasn't acting weird. The super burp was. And *it* never listened to Louie!

"It's Sea Monkey salsa time!" George shouted out. His feet began to move back and forth. "One, two, three. One, two, three," he counted as he danced.

Everyone laughed harder. Even the Kangaroos were cracking up.

Mrs. Kelly danced along with him. George took her by the hand and spun her around. He took one of her pom-poms and began whirling it over his head.

George and Mrs. Kelly **were wiggling, jiggling, whirling, and twirling**. And then . . .

Pop! George felt the air rush right out of him.

Drop. George fell to the ground.

Kerplop. Mrs. Kelly landed on her butt.

George opened his mouth to say, **"Hi, Mrs. Kelly."** And that's exactly what came out.

"Hi, George," Mrs. Kelly said with a gummy grin. She straightened her glasses and wiped a huge bead of sweat from her forehead.

Crack! Just then George heard a loud noise coming from the field. Louie had just hit a fly ball! The Kangaroos' right fielder should have been able to catch it. But he was **still laughing** about George and Mrs. Kelly dancing around. The ball flew over his glove and landed just near the fence.

"Woo-hoo!" George heard Julianna shout from the dugout. "Come on, Louie! That's at least a double!"

George grinned. He knew that if it hadn't been for him, Louie would have been out for sure. He also knew that Louie would never, ever admit that. But that didn't matter. The Sea Monkeys were back in the game.

"And now, I present to you, this year's fourth-grade baseball champions— the Edith B. Sugarman Elementary Sea

Monkeys!" Principal McKeon began clapping and then she placed the **shiny new trophy** in the case in the front of the school.

Chris, struggling to carry his huge sculpture, walked up behind her. "And here's our mascot!" he said proudly as he put the sculpture next to the trophy case.

Everyone started cheering. "Sea Monkeys! Sea Monkeys! Sea Mo—"

Crrraaaccckk. Suddenly the tail cracked right off the sea-monkey mascot.

"Oh no!" Chris exclaimed. He looked at the mascot. "Hey! There's gum on my sculpture. *Already-been-chewed* gum." He stared at Alex. **"Did you do this?"**

George's stomach flip-flopped. He wasn't sure what to do. If he told the truth, both of his best friends would be mad at him; Chris for his breaking the sculpture and Alex for his taking the gum.

But George couldn't let Alex take the blame for something he hadn't done.

"It was me," George said slowly. "I broke the sculpture. But I tried to fix it—with some of Alex's gum. And it worked—for a while."

Chris and Alex stared at George.

"*You* broke my sculpture?" Chris asked.

"Not on purpose," George assured him.

"*You* stole my ABC gum?" Alex asked.

"I was gonna replace it." George pulled some ABC gum from his pocket. "Here's a really big glob. Six pieces! There's only a little pocket lint on it."

Alex took the glob of gum. "Okay," he said. "This is more gum than you took. It should fix things."

"It won't fix my sculpture," Chris said sadly.

"But I can," Mrs. Jasper told Chris. "I have glue that's made especially for clay.

Your mascot will be as good as new."

Chris smiled.

"I'm sorry," George apologized.

"It's okay," Chris said. "Friends make mistakes."

George nodded. Did they *ever*! George had made *a lot* of mistakes in the past few days. He was lucky he still had *any* friends.

"Let me get a picture," Louie's mom shouted. "Everyone gather near the trophy. Loo Loo Poo, you stand right in the middle."

George laughed.

"I don't understand why this team doesn't have a Most Valuable Player award," Mrs. Farley complained to Coach Trainer and Principal McKeon.

"Everyone on this team is valuable," Coach Trainer explained to her. "They were all responsible for the win."

"But my Louie was *more* responsible," Mrs. Farley argued. "He made a great hit."

"And at least two lousy errors," George whispered to Julianna and Alex.

"Loo Loo Poo, if there was an MVP award, you would have earned it," his mother told him.

George shook his head. That wasn't true. The real reason the team had won was that the Kangaroos **couldn't help laughing** whenever they saw George— which was every time they went up to bat.

It's really hard to keep your eye on the ball when you're laughing! After George's big dance show, the Kangaroo players had struck out—*a lot*.

So actually, when he thought about it, if there was going to be a **most valuable player**, it would have to be the super burp. But that didn't mean George wanted to keep on burping. No way. George really wanted to lose that burp. The sooner, the better.

About the Author

Nancy Krulik is the author of more than 150 books for children and young adults including three *New York Times* best sellers and the popular Katie Kazoo, Switcheroo books. She lives in New York City with her family, and many of George Brown's escapades are based on things her own kids have done. (No one delivers a good burp quite like Nancy's son, Ian!) Nancy's favorite thing to do is laugh, which comes in pretty handy when you're trying to write funny books!

About the Illustrator

Aaron Blecha was raised by a school of giant squid in Wisconsin and now lives with his family by the English seaside. He works as an artist designing toys, animating cartoons, and illustrating books, including the Zombiekins and The Rotten Adventures of Zachary Ruthless series. You can enjoy more of his weird creations at www.monstersquid.com.